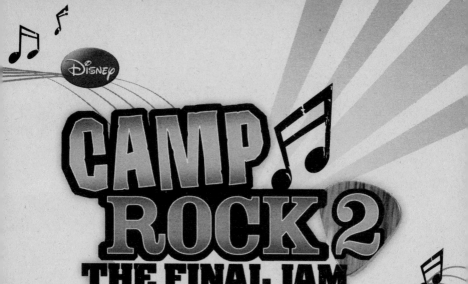

CAMP ROCK 2
THE FINAL JAM

The Junior Novel

Adapted by Wendy Loggia
Based on "Camp Rock: The Final Jam,"
Written by Dan Berendsen and Karin Gist & Regina Hicks
Based on Characters Created by Karin Gist & Regina Hicks
and Julie Brown & Paul Brown

DISNEP PRE
New York

CHAPTER 1

Mitchie Torres's forehead pressed against the window of her mom's van, willing her to drive faster. Pine trees, rest stops, more pine trees . . . the trip seemed like it was taking forever! Then, suddenly, they came around a curve in the road, and Mitchie let out a scream.

"There's the sign! Turn! Turn!" she told her mom excitedly as the wooden Camp Rock marker came into view. "I can't believe we're finally here." Mitchie had been dreaming about being back at the prestigious musical camp all year long—and finally she was!

She searched her bag frantically for her phone. "I told Shane I'd text him when we were almost there," Mitchie said.

Connie, Mitchie's mom and Camp Rock's cook extraordinaire, looked over at her. "Mitchie . . ." she began, before breaking off.

Mitchie stopped her search. "What?" she asked.

Her mom sighed. "Nothing."

Mitchie gave her mom a questioning look. "Well, it's obviously something," she said, having noticed the caution in her mom's voice. "You and subtle—not very good friends."

Connie hesitated. "I know you and Shane talk all the time, but you haven't actually seen this boy in almost a year," she told her daughter gently. "I don't want you to be too disappointed if he can't come this summer."

"Mom!" Mitchie felt exasperated. She knew

her mom was just trying to protect her, but she was positive that Shane Gray would be there. Sure, he was the famous lead singer of Connect 3, but he'd also gotten his start at Camp Rock. After all, his uncle Brown Cesario was the camp's director. Mitchie and Shane had been e-mailing and texting each other all year. Mitchie had no doubt; Shane would definitely be back for another summer.

"I just want you to have fun and focus on your music," Connie finished as they approached the camp's driveway.

Mitchie took a deep breath. "First, this is going to be the best summer ever. And second, nothing could ever make me lose my—" She stopped midsentence to gape out the window. "What's that?"

Across the road was a brand-new flashing neon sign that read CAMP STAR. It had a silhouette of a girl singing into a microphone, surrounded by musical notes. It pointed in the direction opposite Camp Rock.

Mitchie couldn't believe it. Did someone open another music camp?

Everything at Camp Rock was the same as Mitchie remembered. Bright sunshine, rustic cabins with cozy porches, the fresh smell of pine in the air, the beach, and the beautiful lake.

She hoisted her duffel bag out of the van. "Seriously, why would somebody open another music camp right across the lake?" she asked, shaking her head. That didn't make any sense. Everyone knew that Camp Rock was the *only* camp for aspiring rock stars.

Connie shrugged. "Who knows? But I don't think it's anything to worry about. Maybe . . ."

But Mitchie wasn't listening. She'd just spotted one of the greatest things about Camp Rock— her best friend, Caitlyn Gellar!

Squealing, Mitchie ran over to hug her. "I was afraid we'd be late, but it doesn't look like too many people are here yet," she said.

Caitlyn grinned. She was a little taller, maybe,

but other than that she looked exactly the same. "You know what this means," Caitlyn said, grabbing her own luggage and pulling Mitchie toward their old cabin. "Since we're the first ones here, we totally get our choice of bunk."

Caitlyn and Mitchie swung open the cabin door . . . and stared. Apparently they weren't the first ones there. The cabin was already covered with clothes, shoes, toiletries, and tons of other stuff. And there were three people unpacking —Ella Pador, Peggy "Dupree" Warburton, and camp diva Tess Tyler.

Mitchie and Caitlyn raced inside. The five girls hadn't been together since last summer, and they were excited to be bunkmates this year. Everyone began hugging and screaming and talking all at once.

"Peggy! How was the song? Did you love it?" Mitchie asked her friend, remembering an e-mail Peggy had sent about a song she recorded last month. "I'm sure you were fantastic!"

Peggy was jumping up and down. "It was so

fabulous. I got to record, and they gave me the tape!"

"Ahhh, look at that dress!" Ella exclaimed to Mitchie, stepping back to drink in her fashion choice. "You are so cute!"

Mitchie laughed, then motioned toward Caitlyn. "She won, like, this huge dance competition," she proudly told the girls as Caitlyn tried to shush her. "I'll send you the link. She was so amazing!"

The girls were too busy catching up to notice Tess standing off to the side with her arms crossed. "I see that no one wants to know about *my* life," Tess said, flipping her blond hair over her shoulder. Nothing's changed, Mitchie thought, suppressing a laugh. Tess is still as dramatic as ever!

"What don't we know?" Caitlyn asked. "You update your status, like, every two seconds."

Peggy nodded. "You just tweeted me that Mitchie and Caitlyn are at the cabin door. I'm sitting right next to you."

"Okay, fine," Tess said breezily. "But I have a question. And it's for Mitchie."

Knowing Tess, Mitchie wasn't sure that was a good thing. Tess was a great performer—her mother was rock legend T.J. Tyler—and she was very competitive. "For me?" Mitchie said warily.

Tess smirked. "For you." Then she broke into a wide smile. "What's going on with you and Shane?"

Mitchie felt herself blushing as her friends gathered around her to hear the latest news. "Nothing is going on," she told them, embarrassed to be the center of attention.

"Total lie," Caitlyn declared.

But Mitchie shook her head. "You're all obsessed. But seriously, unless we actually get to spend some time together, nothing is ever going to happen."

And they would only get to see each other if Shane actually returned to Camp Rock.

He would be there . . . wouldn't he?

Shane Gray was the lead singer of one of the

hottest bands on the planet. But right now? He was sweaty, greasy, and completely out of breath. He and his brothers, Nate and Jason, were on their way to Camp Rock when their tour bus got a flat tire.

"One more crank and I think we're good to go," Shane said, putting all his weight into the lug wrench in his hand. He pushed the tire. Nothing. So he pulled. Still nothing. "That's probably fine," he said, feeling less confident than he sounded.

His brothers stood alongside him, their arms crossed. Their bus driver, Oliver, had collapsed, exhausted, on a nearby rock.

"Can we please just wait for the tow truck?" Nate asked, giving the tire a skeptical look. "Oliver tried and he couldn't do it."

Shane struggled to get the wrench off the bolt. "That's because Oliver wasn't properly motivated," he said, huffing. "He's not trying to get to Camp Rock before Mitchie."

Shane had met Mitchie last summer at Camp

Rock. At first, he had fallen in love with her voice. When he met Mitchie, he hadn't even realized *she* was the girl behind the voice. They'd become good friends. And at the end of camp—after much drama—they'd become boyfriend and girlfriend. They'd stayed in touch all year, and Shane couldn't wait to see her.

"Maybe because Oliver doesn't even know Mitchie," Jason pointed out.

Nate walked over, and to Shane's surprise, easily took the wrench off the bolt.

"Thank you," Shane said, relieved that they could finally be on their way again. He and the guys walked toward the front of the bus as Oliver started to lower the jack.

"It's going to be so cool!" Shane said excitedly. "I've got it all planned. She's going to come in, and I'll just be sitting there, and I'll go, 'Hey, Mitchie.' She's going to be so surprised."

Nate looked at him. "'Hey, Mitchie.' That's your big line?"

Shane was confident. "Trust me, everything's

cool when *I* do it. I'm just looking forward to actually, *finally*, getting to spend a little time with her."

"Oh, wait!" Jason blurted out, reaching in his pocket. "I almost forgot. Here." He handed Shane a bolt.

"Is this from the tire?" Shane asked, staring at it.

"Yeah, I saw it on the ground, and I put it in my pocket so we wouldn't lose it," Jason said. "It looks kind of important."

"You don't think you could have mentioned this before?" Shane asked, slightly worried. He didn't know anything about auto mechanics, but the bolt had to have been there for a reason.

"How could I mention it before now if I didn't remember it until now?" Jason asked, shrugging.

Shane glanced over to the tire as Oliver pulled out the jack. Everything was fine. "It's okay. One bolt's not going to matter," Shane said, trying to sound convincing.

All of a sudden, the tire fell off. Then the back corner of the tour bus crashed to the ground, making a sickening thud.

"Oh, no!" Shane cried, staring in horror. "Please, no. . . ."

His worst fears were realized as the entire bus tipped over. *Kaboom!* The band watched in shock as the bus flipped again and again, rolling down the hill. Finally, with one more deafening boom, it came to a stop.

"See?" Jason said, breaking the silence. "I knew the bolt was important."

Inside Mitchie's cabin, the girls were busy unpacking. Pillows, sweatshirts, hair accessories—it was like a giant sleepover. Mitchie reached into her bag, pulled out her well-worn songbook, and tossed it on her bed. Last summer she'd improved her singing and dancing skills, but her main passion had been— and still was—songwriting.

"I sure hope you have something we can do

at Opening Jam in there," Peggy said. "'Cause if not, we've got nothing."

Mitchie bit her lip, feeling a bit shy about her work. "Kind of, maybe. I don't know. I just started working on something."

She flipped to a page and began to sing some lines she'd written a few days ago. Then she stopped. "That's as far as I got," she said. "I have some more lyrics, but I haven't worked it all out yet."

Ella perched on her bed. "Maybe we could just sing that first part over and over again."

Before Mitchie could respond she heard a guitar playing outside, followed by drumsticks tapping out a beat on the cabin wall.

"That's it!" Mitchie cried, hopping up.

"Really?" Ella said, happily surprised. "Nobody ever agrees with me."

But Mitchie wasn't answering Ella. Instead, she'd realized that the beat she was hearing belonged to two of her best friends from last summer, Barron James and Sander Loya!

She rushed outside and threw her arms around their shoulders. "I knew that was you guys!"

Mitchie looked at her friends' smiling faces and grinned. It felt awesome to be back at Camp Rock, back at a place where she could live and breathe music with people who felt the same way she did.

CHAPTER 2

Camp Rock's jams were legendary, and this summer's Opening Jam did not disappoint. Mitchie felt incredible being on the Camp Rock main stage again, and her voice sounded clear and strong as she finished her song with her friends.

"Rock on, Camp Rock!" she yelled into the mike before handing it over to Brown Cesario, Camp Rock's enthusiastic director and founding member of the classic rock band the Wet Crows. The crowd was still wildly applauding Mitchie as Brown began to address the campers.

"Mitchie Torres, returning rocker!" he said, smiling over at Mitchie appreciatively and running his fingers through his dirty blond hair. "Welcome to the heart and soul of rock and roll. Whether you're slick and happenin' or dark and jammin', Camp Rock is the place to be." He gazed out at the campers' attentive faces. "Now, I'm sure you've noticed there aren't quite as many of you as in years past, but not to worry—"

Suddenly he was cut off. Mitchie had grabbed his arm. "Shane!" she shouted, rushing off the stage.

"Sorry," Connie muttered to Brown. "She does that."

But who could blame her? Mitchie had just spotted Shane, Jason, and Nate pulling up to the camp . . . in the back of a farmer's pickup truck?

Mitchie gaped as Shane's adorable face

appeared, surrounded by hay and a few chicken crates.

"Hey, Mitchie!" he called . . . before falling out of the back of the truck.

"Shane!" Mitchie cried again, running over to him and helping him to his feet. Someone had tied his shoelaces together. She shot a dirty look toward Jason and Nate. She had a pretty good idea it was one of them. "Are you all right?" she asked Shane. A chicken landed on his head, and Mitchie giggled.

"I'm fine," he said as the chicken hopped off. He grinned sheepishly at her. "Surprise."

"Surprise," Mitchie said, smiling back at him. She had waited so long for this moment, and now that it was here she didn't know where to begin.

The guys grabbed their luggage and, along with Mitchie, began walking toward Brown, who waved them over.

"Yes, Rockers, my nephews and Camp Rock alum, better known to the world as Connect 3, are going to be with us for the summer," he announced. "The official reason being they missed their uncle, but somehow I don't think that's the whole story."

Mitchie looked over at Shane. "The summer? Really?" With Connect 3's busy schedule, she'd been hoping they would be there for a month at the most. Knowing that she and Shane would have all summer together was awesome!

"I already know it's not going to be long enough," Shane said, gazing at Mitchie. Her heart skipped a beat.

"People staring. You should probably react," Jason muttered. "Wave. Blink."

Laughing, Mitchie and Shane finally stopped looking at each other and faced the other campers.

"Hey, Rockers," Shane said, giving a wave. "I'm Shane. This is Nate and Jason. I know it'll be hard, but just treat us like any other camper."

The crowd of kids smiled, then turned back to listen to Brown, still on the stage.

"So maybe it won't be that hard," Shane said as Mitchie laughed.

"As I was saying," Brown continued, "we're a little smaller this year, and that's courtesy of our new friends across the lake—Camp Star. Founded, not so coincidentally, by my out-to-destroy-me, still-mad-that-I-kicked-him-out-of-the-group former bandmate, Axel Turner."

Shane, Jason, and Nick let out a simultaneous low groan.

"That was like a hundred years ago," Jason said.

"Twenty-five," Brown corrected. "But thank you for that."

Tess was hopping up and down in the crowd. "Axel Turner? The guy who owns Star Records?" she said excitedly. "You mean he's right across the lake?"

Mitchie shot her a look. The girl sounded way too excited about Camp Star.

"Yes," Brown said, answering Tess's question.

"And I share your disdain," he added sarcastically. "Now, it's going to take some effort, but I'm sure that we can all peacefully coexist on the lake without—"

Just then a sleek speedboat with a Camp Star flag on its stern roared across the lake. It was so loud it drowned out Brown's words.

As it circled back around for a second pass, a small cannon on the boat's deck fired four times.

"Get down!" Jason shouted. "We're under attack!"

Four parachutes sailed out of the cannon and opened up to reveal little baskets. The Camp Rockers watched as they floated down into the crowd.

"It's full of marshmallows!" Peggy exclaimed, catching one.

"This one has chocolate," Caitlyn said, holding another.

"Graham crackers," Barron said, wagging his eyebrows.

"And who made these parachutes?" Ella wanted to know. "They're adorable!"

Mitchie opened a note that was attached to one of the baskets. "'The whole camp is invited to an opening-night bonfire,'" she read. Everyone began cheering.

Brown was shaking his head. "No. Absolutely not. I know this guy. This is a setup. For what, I'm not sure—well, cavities for one—but trust me, no good can come of this."

But by the reaction of all the campers, Brown had clearly lost control. Kids were standing up, talking excitedly about the bonfire, and heading down to the beach to get the canoes ready.

"It'll be fun," Connie said, trying to reassure Brown. "You just said we have to try and get along. And I'm not just saying that because I haven't made anything for dessert yet."

Brown let out a sigh. No dessert *and* Axel Turner inviting his campers to a bonfire? This was bad. Really bad.

* * *

Mitchie sucked in her breath as her canoe pulled up to the Camp Star docks. She didn't really care about the bonfire—but she was curious to see what Camp Star was all about.

And as she gazed up the hill, she had a pretty good idea.

The place didn't look like a camp—it was a resort!

She noticed that behind her, Shane was having a little trouble. As in, he had one foot on the dock while his other foot was still in his boat. And the boat was starting to drift.

"A little help?" Shane was calling to his brothers, who were already on their way to the camp.

Laughing, Mitchie reached out and grabbed Shane, pulling him to safety. "See?" she said. "These are the kinds of things I can't learn about you over e-mail."

"Maybe we should go back to that," Shane

joked. "Unless you found that sweet and endearing instead of stupid and klutzy."

Definitely sweet, Mitchie thought. She couldn't wait to spend some quality time with Shane. But finding out what Camp Star was up to came first.

Farther down the dock, a group of rowdy nine-year-old Junior Camp Rockers was getting out of their boat. Their counselor, a harried looking guy with a bad sunburn, was trying to get them in line.

Jason walked over to them. "I remember when I was a Junior Rocker," he said, feeling nostalgic. He pumped his fist. "Rock on, my little brothers. Bumps and high fives."

One of the Junior Rockers was filming all the goings-on with a video camera. "Oh, hey, little man, what do we have here?" Jason said, nodding appreciatively. "A video camera? Very cool."

He reached over to touch it, but the kid pulled away.

"Don't touch it," the boy said, frowning.

Jason's eyes widened. "What, you think I'm going to drop it in the water?"

The kid shrugged, then handed it to Jason . . . who accidentally dropped it in the water.

"And if you thought that, you'd have been right," Jason said, taking a deep breath as the boy crossed his arms and scowled up at him.

Meanwhile, Brown and Connie had started walking up the path, but had been stopped by Brown's former bandmate—now nemesis—Axel Turner.

"Brown, my man," Axel said, grinning. "Long time."

Brown sighed. "And yet never long enough. Look, Axel, I don't know what you're playing at—"

Axel held up his hands "Whoa! I'm beginning to remember why I left the band."

"Left the band?" Brown exclaimed. "*You* left the band? Is that what you're telling people?" Axel had been thrown out of the band for a bad attitude that went beyond normal rock-star behavior. The guy was talented for sure—but completely ruthless.

"You, my friend, have got to stop living in the past," Axel declared. "I'm trying to reach out to you here."

Brown couldn't believe his ears. "By driving me out of business?"

Axel smiled again. "There's no reason we both can't be successful. We each have our niche."

"Niche?" Brown repeated warily.

"Camp Star is dedicated to producing the superstars of tomorrow. What's your place about again?" Axel asked, as if he didn't know.

"Encouraging kids in their love of music," Brown said firmly. And if that led to them becoming professional musicians, even better. Focusing on their craft—songwriting, producing, dancing, singing—not aiming for instant superstardom was what Brown was all about.

Axel smiled as he turned to go. "Like I said, room for both of us."

Brown turned to Connie. "Just to be clear, he did not leave the band. We kicked him out."

"I know," Connie assured him. "It's okay."

But it wasn't okay. Brown was seriously worried. How would Camp Rock compete with superslick Camp Star?

CHAPTER 3

Up near the Camp Star amphitheater, Nate was leaning against the railing, staring out into the darkness.

Jason walked up to him. "Ready?"

Nate shook his head. "No. We shouldn't be here. It's so obvious this guy is just doing this to get back at Brown," he said. "First he tries to take down the Wet Crows and now Camp Rock." Nate glanced at the Camp Star mug in

Jason's hand. "What is that?" he asked.

"Hot chocolate. They're handing it out for free. And you get to keep the mug," Jason replied.

Nate stared at his brother.

"What?" Jason said, wide-eyed.

"There's no way I'm going to this bonfire," Nate said firmly.

Just then a pretty girl walked by. As Nate gazed after her in awe, she turned to smile at them.

"Hey, pouty boy, you better hurry!" the girl called. "The bonfire's about to start."

Nate watched her go, then realized Jason was looking at him. "We should probably go," he said, forgetting all about his earlier decision. "I think the bonfire is about to start." Without waiting for an answer, he started walking briskly up the path in the same direction the gorgeous girl had just gone.

"Don't mock," Nate said over his shoulder before Jason could call him out.

"I'm not mocking," Jason said, stifling a laugh.

"Yes you are."

Jason pushed aside a branch. "Maybe a little."

Everyone was filing into the Camp Star amphitheater. Mitchie was looking for her friends when Shane came jogging over and pulled her aside.

"Question," he said, looking into her eyes. "What do you say, later on, you and I break away and finally go on a real first date?"

Mitchie smiled. "Answer. I'd like that." She looked over at the huge amphitheater stage. "Wow," she murmured, her eyes flitting from the lights to the speakers. It was hard not to be impressed.

"I know, right?" Tess chimed in, walking past. "That's all I've been saying since I got off the boat."

Mitchie slipped her hand in Shane's and together they found seats next to Ella. The place was filling up quickly with people from both camps.

"So I thought this was supposed to be a campfire," Mitchie said, looking around. There was no campfire in sight. "Singing, telling stories, an actual fire . . . "

Suddenly the lights went off. Axel Turner walked out onto the stage. "If everyone could take their seats," he said into his mike. He cleared his throat. "Hi, I'm Axel Turner, and I'd like to welcome all you Rockers and my dear old friend Brown Cesario to Camp Star!"

Mitchie rolled her eyes. Dear old friend? He seemed more like a mortal enemy from what she'd heard.

"But you all don't want to hear a speech from me," Axel went on. "You want to get to what a campfire is really all about, singing."

Ella elbowed Mitchie. "Hey, that's what you just said. You're twins!"

"So, does anyone have anything they'd like to play?" Axel continued. "Camp Rockers, no need to be shy." He paused for a moment, but nobody volunteered. "No takers?" Axel asked. "Well, no worries. Camp Star will start us off. And apologies if we embarrass ourselves. We're kind of new at this."

"Does somebody want to use my guitar?" Mitchie spoke up, glancing around. She hadn't noticed anyone else with an instrument.

"No," Axel told her. "I think we're good." He pointed off stage and . . . bam! The whole stage lit up. Startled, Mitchie fell back into her seat as lights began blinking and a base line began thumping.

A tall, good-looking young guy about Shane's age walked out on the stage as if he owned it. As he started to sing, a full chorus of Camp Star backup singers and dancers strutted across the stage.

Mitchie looked at Shane, who was just as dumbfounded as she was. Forget a "campfire." This was like being at a Connect 3 concert! What was going on?

The guy continued to belt out the lyrics, stopping for a moment as the spotlight shifted to a girl playing the keyboard. She was amazing.

As the song ended, a final showy blast of pyrotechnics burst across the front of the stage. Then the girl on the keyboard threw her hands up in the air with a flourish. A gold bracelet flew off her wrist and into the crowd.

"Ow! My eye!" Nate cried out as the bracelet hit him in the face.

Mitchie and the Camp Rockers all looked a little shell-shocked. Mitchie applauded politely. She wasn't sure what to think of the spectacle she'd just witnessed.

Tess jumped to her feet, whooping and whistling. "Whoooooooo! That was so good!" She glanced at Mitchie. "Wasn't that good? That was good!"

Before Mitchie could respond, Axel came back out onstage. "And that's how we do things at Camp Star. Before we go further, I just wanted to make a quick announcement. We're having some staffing problems. Who knew we'd be so popular?"

Brown had walked over to Shane and Mitchie.

"What's he doing?" Shane asked.

"We really are under attack," Brown said, not taking his eyes off the stage.

"So I'm just going to put it out there," Axel continued. "If there are any Camp Rock counselors or staff who'd like to make the switch, I'd be more than willing to double your salary."

Brown was furious. "I barely have enough staff as it is!"

Mitchie gasped as Camp Rock counselors began calling out.

"I'll go," said one.

"Me, too," said a counselor Mitchie recognized from the dock. More people raised their hands. It was mass desertion!

Two Camp Star counselors holding clipboards stood next to Axel on the stage. "And if there are any campers who'd like to join us, well, I'm sure we could find you a bunk. Did I mention our cabins are air-conditioned?"

Now it was pandemonium as campers and counselors alike started talking excitedly.

Outraged, Mitchie leaped to her feet. "He can't do that!"

Brown grabbed Jason's arm. "I need all Camp Rockers back on the boats. Now."

Jason was angry. "Dude, we can't just let him get away with this!"

"Later!" Brown barked. "Just go."

Mitchie hurried off to help gather up the Camp Rockers. This is supposed to be the best summer of my life, Mitchie thought, waving a few campers over. And I'm not about to sit by and watch Axel Turner ruin it!

"**A**re you sure it's okay?" Nate asked his brother. They were standing by the side of the stage and Shane was examining his eye.

"Not even a scratch," Shane assured him, patting his arm.

"I'm really sorry about that," a girl's voice said. Nate spun around. It was the pretty girl he had noticed before—who had also ended up being an amazing keyboard player.

"It's cool," Nate said nonchalantly. "I'm totally fine. Just happy I could catch it for you."

She smiled. "Well, it's always kinda been my lucky charm. Guess it still works."

"Did you miss the part where it hit him in the eye?" Shane blurted out. Then, noticing Nate's annoyed look, he began backing up. "Hey, I think I'm going to go walk around aimlessly. See ya."

Now it was just Nate and the girl. Feeling tongue-tied, Nate looked down at the bracelet in his hand. "So . . . 'Onop,'" he said, trying to read the letters.

She turned it around in his hand.

"So, *Dana*," he corrected himself, feeling like an idiot. "That actually makes more sense. You were really good."

She blushed. "You think? I'm just glad it's finally over," she confessed. "I've been practicing for weeks. Right before I went on I was almost sure I was going to throw up." She paused. "So, Nate . . ."

"How'd you know my name?" Nate asked her.

"Uh, because I'd, like, have to live under a rock to not know that," Dana said as if it were obvious. "It's got to be so incredible. You know, not just being you, but being in a band. Traveling around the world. I'd love that. Maybe not the band part—but at least the traveling part."

Nate nodded. "Yeah, it's pretty cool."

An awkward moment of silence passed between them. Nate wanted to say something interesting or cool, but the words just weren't coming.

"I'm really glad you guys came," Dana said finally. "My dad was totally sure that none of you would show."

Nate gave her a quizzical glance.

"My dad's Axel Turner," she explained.

"He's your dad?" Nate couldn't believe this girl was that guy's daughter.

"Everybody says that. And kind of just like that," she said ruefully. "But trust me, once you get to know him he's a really great guy."

Nate wasn't too sure about that. He also wasn't sure what to say next. He stared down at the bracelet.

"Well, I should probably go," Dana said at last.

"Here," Nate said, holding out the bracelet. "You don't want to lose it."

"You can keep it if you want," Dana said.

"What would I do with a bracelet?" Nate asked before he could stop himself.

"Right," Dana said, nodding quickly. "And for the record, I'm glad you're okay. You've got really pretty eyes." She looked suddenly self-conscious. "I'm sorry. That was weird. I didn't mean to make you uncomfortable."

"Don't worry about it," Nate told her. "People talk about them all the time. You know, they're right there in the middle of my face, so . . ."

"So . . . see ya around," Dana said, turning on her heel and hurrying off.

Nate watched her go and then smacked himself in the head. *"Aaah!"* he exclaimed. There were so many things he should have told her! "You have pretty eyes, too! Yes, I want to keep it. I want to put it under my pillow and look at it every day. Stupid. Stupid!" he said aloud to himself. Then Nate stalked off, passing Shane. "I'm an idiot," he muttered.

"Great. Finally something we can agree on," Shane said.

Nate strode back and punched him.

"Ow! A very strong idiot!" Shane cried, rubbing his arm.

Meanwhile, Dana's father had caught up to her. "I don't want you talking to that boy," he told her sternly.

"Don't worry," she said, dejected. "I don't think it's going to be a problem."

CHAPTER 4

Rounding up the other Camp Rockers wasn't easy. For the past fifteen minutes, Mitchie had gone from classroom to classroom at Camp Star looking for campers. She opened the door to the recording studio. Two campers were inside, singing.

"Rockers. Boats. Two minutes," she told them. The girls hesitated—then bolted out the door.

Mitchie gazed around. "Wow," she whispered, taking in all the expensive, state-of-the-art equipment. "Now that's a recording studio." As she turned to go outside she bumped smack into the guy who'd just performed like a bona fide rock star—with the attitude to match.

"Hey," he said, smiling broadly at her.

"Hi," Mitchie said flatly. She was not interested in talking to him. But he wouldn't move out of her way. "Can I help you with something?" she asked, raising an eyebrow.

"Do I look like I need any help?" he asked slyly.

"Do I know you?" Mitchie said. Then she raised her voice, calling out, "Boats. Two minutes!"

The guy laughed. "Do you know me? That's a good one." He gazed at her. "I'm Luke. Luke Williams? I was just onstage, like, two minutes ago." He started singing a few lines of the song from before. "That's what I'm talking about."

Mitchie rolled her eyes. "Oh, yeah. Impressive."

"I know, right?" Luke said, not picking up on her sarcasm. "So, you thinking about joining us over here?"

"Uh, no," Mitchie said, attempting to brush past him. "I'm good where I am, thanks."

Luke smirked. "Yeah, well, you're Shane Gray's girlfriend so . . ."

Mitchie stopped. "Wait. What does Shane . . . That is not . . . How do you even know that?"

"You gotta know the players if you want to be in the game," Luke said smugly. "Am I right?"

"No."

"It's a tough business," Luke said, his eyes narrowing into slits.

Mitchie stared at him. "It's summer camp."

"To you," Luke pointed out. "For anybody at Camp Star, it's step one to a long and illustrious career. I don't have time for second-rate."

"We're not second-rate," Mitchie argued.

"You don't have to get all defensive," Luke told her, holding up his hands. "You don't have to try and convince *me*."

"I'm not *trying* to do anything," Mitchie said, glaring at him.

"Good. Then Camp Rock is the perfect place for you."

Mitchie felt as if she was about to explode. "Look, just so we're clear, Luke 'I'm giving you the fiiiiiiiiire' Williams, there isn't a single Camp Rocker, not one, who would ever in a million years think about coming to this narcissistic, overproduced ego factory!" she burst out.

Just then Tess ran over, holding up her phone. "Guess what? My mom said yes. I get to switch!" she exclaimed.

Luke beamed. "That's great. Welcome to the ego factory."

Tess beamed back. "Thanks!"

Mitchie stared at her. "Tess, how could you?"

Tess put on a sad face. "I know. I'm sorry. I feel horrible, but—" Suddenly she was smiling again. "Who am I kidding? I'm so excited I can't even pretend to be sympathetic!" Tess touched Luke's arm. "I love what you just

41

did up there," she gushed. "So impressive!"

"I know, right?" Luke bragged. "It's kinda my thing."

Mitchie had had enough. "Good luck finding a spotlight big enough for both of you," she said before storming off. She couldn't wait to get back to Camp Rock.

It was only a mile away . . . but a world apart.

As the sun rose the next day, everyone who had decided to stay on at Camp Rock gathered in the mess hall. Mitchie stood in the middle of a crowd of campers, while Sander and Barron were at a DJ table behind her.

"Everything's going to be fine," Mitchie was assuring the campers. "Brown's a smart guy. He'll figure it out."

"Thanks for that vote of confidence."

Mitchie looked up to see the camp director standing just inside the mess-hall doorway. "I guess there's no need for me to get everyone's attention," he said. He looked really tired—as if he'd been up all night long. He gazed out at the campers. "The good news is—and this seriously warms my heart—we lost very few campers last night."

"Tess," Mitchie muttered, scowling. She knew Tess was super competitive and serious about her career, but she still couldn't believe she'd walked away from her two BFFs, Ella and Peggy, and defected from Camp Rock.

"I am *so* defriending her," Ella declared.

"But we did lose quite a few of our remaining staff," Brown continued, rubbing his temples. "Which means . . . I can't believe I'm going to say this . . . Camp Rock is closed. Effective immediately."

Mitchie was stunned. Close Camp Rock? He couldn't be serious! But by the looks of the grim faces around her, he was.

"You have to believe me," Brown said over the campers' disappointed protests, "I truly have no other choice. I'll start calling parents as soon as we're done here . . . which, I guess, is now. I'm sorry." With an abrupt nod, he walked quickly out of the mess hall, leaving the room in chaos.

"Brown!" Shane exclaimed. "Wait!" He grabbed his brothers and together they ran after him.

"Camp is over?" Ella said, dismayed. "But we just got here. It's not fair."

Caitlyn slumped her shoulders. "It's not his fault. There's nothing he can do about it."

Mitchie's mind was racing. "But that doesn't mean there isn't something *we* can do about it," she said, thinking out loud.

"Mitchie—" Peggy began.

"We're not going home!" Mitchie declared, smiling for the first time all morning. "This is our summer. We're not giving up, and we aren't backing down."

All of them—Mitchie, Caitlyn, Peggy, Ella, Sander, Barron, and Shane and his brothers— they were all in this together. Camp Rock was where they'd found their sounds, their voices, their strengths—and each other. There was no way they could just walk away from it all.

They had to take on Camp Star and win this thing.

There was too much at stake if they didn't.

A short while later, Mitchie and her friends walked into Brown's office. They'd all changed into Camp Rock staff T-shirts.

Brown sat at his desk, piles of papers spread out before him. He put down his phone and stared at them. "What is going on?"

Mitchie spoke up. "You said you were short a few counselors. So I found you some new ones."

Please take a chance on us, she thought, her heart pounding. We can do this.

After a moment, Brown's weathered face broke into a smile. "Then it looks like I should call this staff meeting to order."

Mitchie grinned. They wouldn't let him—or Camp Rock—down.

CHAPTER 5

"**N**o. No way!" Jason cried, staring at the class schedule Mitchie had hung up on the message board outside the cabins. He'd been expecting lifeguard duty—or maybe one-on-one lessons with one of the more experienced musicians— but instead he'd been assigned counselor duty for the Junior Rockers!

A bunch of campers gathered around him, snickering. And when Nate and Shane came over and began leading him toward the Junior Rockers' recreation room, he was adamant.

"No way," Jason said, shaking his head. "I already told you, I'm not going to do it." Spend his summer with a bunch of wild kids? Uh-uh. Not happening.

"Jason, you're looking at this all wrong," Nate said. "This isn't a punishment. It's a reward."

"Really?" Jason was doubtful. The job he'd been assigned sure didn't feel like a reward.

"Really," Nate insisted. "It means everyone thinks that you have the leadership skills, the intelligence, the maturity, and the sheer guts to handle this assignment."

Shane gave an appreciative nod. "Wow, you're good," he told Nate.

"Thanks," Nate whispered.

Jason's eyes brightened. Nate had made some excellent points. "You're right," he said slowly, warming to the idea. "This is an honor."

Nate gave a happy smile. "Exactly. Now get

in there and make us proud. We'll be right here if you need us."

Shane handed Jason a clipboard. Squaring his shoulders, Jason headed up the steps to the rec room. He was so busy looking forward that he didn't notice his brothers had taken off running.

As Jason stepped inside, he was greeted by the curious stares of Camp Rock's youngest rockers—including Trevor, the kid whose camera Jason had dropped.

"Hi, kids. Guys. Men," Jason said, stepping forward. "I'm Jason." He glanced at Trevor. "We kind of already . . . You got that new camera I sent over, right?"

The kid nodded.

"Okay, so I am going to be your counselor, and we are going to have a great time together. I have your schedule right . . . It's . . . I must have . . . " He felt inside his pockets. No schedule.

Then he threw his hands up in the air. So

what? "It's camp," he said breezily. "Who needs a schedule?"

"When do we get to rock?" asked a Junior Rocker named Audrey.

Jason smiled. "We'll get to that, but first we need to . . ." He wasn't sure what they needed to do first, actually. "I'm kind of new at this, so go easy on me, okay?"

The kids all looked at one another.

"I say, let's get him!" shouted Gage, one of the Junior Rockers.

The kids were about to tackle a panicky Jason when Trevor stopped them. "Guys! Guys! Hold on a minute."

Jason gave the kid a relieved smile. "Thank you," he said.

Trevor picked up his video camera and turned it on. "Okay. *Now* get him!"

Jason tried to bolt, but the rec room's screen door got in his way. Before he could say "Connect 3," the Junior Rockers had piled on top of him.

This isn't a punishment, this isn't a punishment, Jason told himself as he felt the knees, elbows, and fists of a dozen ready-to-rock campers.

Mitchie had created a master class schedule for the entire camp, with her friends serving as counselors. On paper, everything looked perfect. In reality, though . . . it wasn't so easy.

Caitlyn was going to be the new dance teacher. She'd dressed in dance gear, did some warm-ups, and psyched herself up to teach jazz to a room full of campers. She strutted into the classroom only to find that she was in the drum cabin—with a group of students sitting behind drum sets.

Meanwhile, Nate thought teaching drums would be a piece of cake . . . except he had a classroom filled with dancers.

Ella was completely nervous about the prospect of teaching, but she loved to sing and dance and would do anything to stay at Camp

Rock. She stumbled into a cabin holding her sketch pads and a few bolts of fabric, pulling a dressmaking mannequin alongside her. "Oh," she said, noticing that the room was filled with campers holding electric guitars. Shrugging, she started setting up her stuff.

Peggy's classroom was so jammed with campers she could barely breathe—while Mitchie showed up in the mess hall ready to lead a class in songwriting only to find that she was the only one there.

Back in the Junior Rockers' rec room, Jason ended up building a birdhouse—while hiding out under a desk as the campers ran around like crazy.

Camp Rock had turned into Camp Chaos.

The next day wasn't any better. Jason was still hanging out under the desk working on his birdhouse when suddenly a baseball smashed into it, breaking it into a hundred pieces.

Furious, he stood up. The Junior Rockers

hadn't even noticed—they were still running around like wild animals, using the desks as drums, playing air guitar. . . .

"Enough!" Jason yelled, losing his last shred of patience. "You wanna rock?"

Shocked at the sound of his angry voice, the kids stopped in their tracks.

"Well, you know what? You don't deserve to rock," Jason ranted. "To be a real rocker, you've got to have discipline and order—three things none of you have."

"That's two things," Trevor pointed out.

"Didn't I say control?" Jason barked. "Well, you don't have that either. Why should I show you the first thing about being a rock star if you won't show me the slightest bit of respect?"

The kids immediately sat down. Jason blinked. He couldn't believe his angry pep talk had actually worked. "All right, that's better," he went on sternly. "Who wants to play drums?"

A few hands shot up.

"Who wants to play guitar?"

A few more hands went up.

Jason surveyed the room. "Who wants to do lead vocals?"

A hand shot up. "Then I suggest you buy yourself some tight pants and learn how to play the tambourine," Jason told him, thinking of someone in particular.

"Hey! I heard that!" Shane's voice came from outside the window.

Jason snickered. "Sorry!" Then he looked back at his now-attentive Junior Rockers and rubbed his hands together. They had a lot to learn.

Making sure he was out of sight, Nate walked down to the lakeside, found a good hiding place behind a cluster of trees, and pulled out his binoculars. He held them up to his eyes and scanned the area.

Nothing, nothing . . . bingo! There, across the water at Camp Star, he spotted her. Dana.

Sitting at a lakeside piano, playing a beautiful melody. The music floated across the water, making Nate's breath catch in his throat. He'd never met anyone like her. . . .

"Nate?"

Nate almost dropped his binoculars. "Yeah!" he said, startled. "Yes? What's up . . . *bro*?" He finally realized the voice belonged to his brother Shane.

"What are you doing?" Shane asked, staring at the binoculars.

"I'm, uh, lifeguard duty," Nate stammered. "This schedule is a mess. But you can't be too careful. One last look and . . ."

He held up the binoculars again, gazing across the water toward Camp Star. Dana was just finishing her performance.

"All clear," Nate said to a bewildered Shane before jogging off. If he hurried, he just might catch her.

Mitchie walked into the mess hall with Shane

right behind her. He pulled her overflowing clipboard from her hands.

"So what do I have to do to separate you from your clipboard?" he wanted to know.

Mitchie smiled. He was so cute. It was just— this was so important. She was about to reply when her mother came hurrying out of the kitchen, her cheeks flushed.

"Mitchie, I've just rolled a hundred pounds of raw hamburger all by myself," she said, sounding exasperated. "I told you I needed help."

"That's impossible," Mitchie said, taking back her clipboard. "I know for a fact that I scheduled . . . absolutely no one. Oops."

Brown came in, took one look at Connie's stressed face, and said, "What's going on?"

Connie sighed. "This is not working. The kitchen is a disaster, I've got no help, and yesterday I ordered fifty pounds of black beans for taco night and they delivered fifty cases of beach balls instead."

Mitchie glanced out the window, where

Sander and some other campers were tossing balls in the air. She giggled. "You know your handwriting isn't—"

"It's rock and roll. It's supposed to be chaotic," Brown interrupted. He gave Mitchie a sincere smile. "You're doing great."

"Thank you," she said, taking a deep breath. But she was going to have to do better.

"How about we make a few more adjustments to the schedule?" Brown suggested, taking a look at Mitchie's clipboard. "And Shane," he called over his shoulder, "help Connie with the burgers."

Mitchie knew Shane would not be thrilled about that.

"I would, but I've got this thing," Shane said, backing up.

But Connie was having none of it. "Yeah, right. Let's go, pretty boy."

Mitchie gave Shane a tiny wave as he slowly followed her mom back into the kitchen. She couldn't wait until they could hang out.

First things first, though. She and Brown had a new schedule to work out.

By the next morning, Camp Rock was on track and on time. The new schedules were posted, and Sander and Barron made morning announcements, alerting the campers.

This time when Caitlyn arrived at the dance barn . . . she found a roomful of dancers warming up. In Peggy's cabin, she was thrilled to see campers on their feet, singing their hearts out. Ella had convinced the guitar players that learning about fashion was an important part of career planning. Jason had the Junior Rockers wrapped around his finger as he showed them how to rock out.

And Mitchie, guitar on her lap and songwriting notebook by her side, was sitting with a half-dozen other campers under a tree near the beach, teaching her songwriting class. Across the way, Shane was showing a group of campers how to handle a microphone.

No chaos. No panic. Everything was going according to plan. Mitchie's eyes flitted from group to group, drinking it in. Some people were playing Frisbee. Others were coming out of cabins, talking excitedly about the class they'd just finished. A few campers were even helping Connie unload boxes from her van.

Camp Star had better watch out, Mitchie thought, playing a few chords. Because Camp Rock was back!

CHAPTER 6

*N*ate was finishing up his drum class. "That's right. Keep it up," he said to the drummers. "And now bring it home." As they ended their session with a loud crash of cymbals, Nate nodded.

"Nice. I knew you could do it." He glanced at the clock. "I think it's a little late to start something new, so whaddaya say we all go enjoy some free time."

And there was no question how he was going to spend it.

The campers were still gathering up their stuff when Nate hurried out of the drum cabin, ran down to the dock, kicked off his shoes, and began untying a canoe.

Minutes later he was paddling across the lake toward Camp Star. As he approached, he allowed the canoe to drift for a moment, trying to see if he could spot Dana through the trees.

"There she is," he muttered. Or, at least, he thought it was her. It was kind of hard to tell with all the trees blocking his view.

"What are you doing?"

Nate yelped. He'd thought he was alone—he hadn't realized that Sander and another camper had floated up alongside him on a Jet Ski!

"Why do people keep doing that?" he asked, shaking his head. Just once, he'd like the chance to spy on Dana *alone*.

"Sorry," Sander said, spraying some water on him. "Just doing our part as activities directors."

"What's today's activity?" Nate asked.

Sander let out a mischievous laugh. "Wake-boarding!"

Nate whipped his head around. A camper was bobbing in the water with a wakeboard at the end of a rope. "No! Don't!" Nate cried, realizing what was about to happen.

But it was too late. Sander revved the engine of the Jet Ski and sped forward. Nate's canoe flipped over, tumbling Nate into the lake. *All those swim lessons are about to come in handy,* he thought, grabbing the canoe and starting to swim.

After what seemed like an eternity, Nate reached the lakeshore at Camp Star. Dripping wet, he stumbled out of the water, pulling the still-overturned canoe behind him. He lay down on a large boulder in the sun, exhausted.

"Are you okay?" Dana asked, walking up to him.

Nate nodded, still trying to catch his breath.

"Don't suppose you were coming over here to

see anyone in particular?" she said nonchalantly.

Nate squeezed his eyes shut, mortified. "No. Just getting some . . . exercise."

"Do you play a lot of sports?" Dana asked brightly.

"Canoeing. That's pretty much it," Nate said, not even sure why he was saying that. He *never* canoed.

"I'm not really all that sporty either," Dana told him. "I played soccer when I was little, but who doesn't?" When Nate didn't say anything, she kept right on talking. "I don't know if it counts as a sport, but I'd love to be a dancer— that's kind of my nerdy secret if-I-could-be-anything-that's-what-I'd-be wish. What would you be?"

"Don't know," Nate said, finally catching his breath. "Never thought about it."

Dana smiled. "Probably because if you could be anything, you'd be you." She paused and looked coyly at Nate. "Do you want to hear something totally stupid? I was goofing around

After spending the school year away from Camp Rock—and her friend Caitlyn—Mitchie is psyched to be back!

They might be one of the hottest bands on the planet, but the members of Connect 3 could stand to learn a thing or two about how to change a tire.

There's nothing sweeter than chocolate, graham crackers, and marshmallows. Could Camp Star's bonfire invitation be a genuine peace offering?

Camp Star's kick-off performance, led by Luke, is amazing and over-the-top.

After learning from Brown that Camp Rock is in danger of closing, Mitchie and the other campers rally to the cause.

When the Camp Rockers challenge Camp Star to a Final Jam showdown, Jason and Nate kick it into rock-star mode.

Nate knows that it's important to practice for the Final Jam, but what's summer without a water-balloon fight?

Planning for the Final Jam has become Mitchie's only focus. Maybe she needs to take a break and cool off!

Shane wishes Mitchie had more time to spend with him.

After realizing that her priorities were a little backwards, Mitchie makes it up to Shane.

Falling for a girl from the wrong side of the lake wasn't exactly part of Nate's summer plans.

At the Final Jam, Dana tells her dad that she likes Nate, regardless of which camp he goes to.

Tess and Luke put their differences aside and perform an awesome jaw-dropping number.

Camp Rockers come together for a Final Jam performance that makes the Star campers realize summer camp is about having fun!

and accidentally sorta wrote your name on my hand, but I used permanent ink by mistake." She thrust out her hand to show him.

"No one's ever written my name on their hand before," Nate mumbled, staring. NATE was written on her wrist, just below her DANA bracelet.

Dana pulled her arm back quickly. "Really more my wrist."

Nate reached out for her hand. "Dana?" he said.

"Yeah?"

"Blech!" Suddenly Nate coughed up a mouthful of lake water. "Sorry," he managed to say.

A voice called out from the trees. "Dana?"

Dana looked panicky. "It's my dad! I'm not supposed to be talking to you. Hurry. Go!"

Without sticking around to find out what would happen if he stayed, Nate raced to his overturned canoe and scrambled underneath it.

He heard Axel's footsteps.

"I, um, saw this canoe," Dana told her father, covering.

"You can tell by the peeling paint it's one of theirs," Axel said. "I'll have an attendant fish it out." There was a moment of silence. He asked, "What's that on your wrist?"

"Nothing," Dana said. And with that, they headed off.

As the sound of their voices faded away, Nate came out from his hiding place. "You know what I want to be?" he said, kicking the ground in frustration. "The kind of guy who can tell you how I really feel. I hate canoes!"

His wet clothes sticking to him, Nate climbed into the canoe, grabbed a paddle, and headed back across the lake to Camp Rock. When he finally arrived, returned the canoe, and began slogging up the hill toward his cabin, there was Shane, drinking it all in.

"I'm still an idiot," Nate muttered as he walked past.

"And I still agree," Shane said.

Nate turned, ready to punch him, but Shane held him off. "Dude, do you mind? You can't keep hitting me."

Nate sighed. His brother was right.

But Shane wasn't safe. Just then, Mitchie came running toward him, tackling him to the ground.

"*Aaah!*" she shrieked excitedly. "I had absolutely the best day! Everything is finally starting to work."

As Nate walked off in search of dry clothes, Shane and Mitchie got up.

"That's great," Shane said. "And it's all because of you."

"Because of us," Mitchie corrected, her eyes sparkling.

"So, now that everyone else has gotten your time, I think I'm going to have to demand some of my own," Shane said, squeezing her hand.

Mitchie squeezed back. "It hasn't been bad."

Shane snorted. "The whole reason I'm here— that my brothers are here—is so I can get to know you a little better," he told her. "But I feel like I've hardly had two seconds alone with you."

Mitchie couldn't believe how cool Shane was being. "That's, like, the sweetest thing anyone's ever said to me."

"But . . . ?" Shane said, raising an eyebrow.

"But—" Mitchie began.

"And now a word from your friendly neighborhood announcer," came Barron's voice over the Camp Rock loudspeaker. "Will the counselors scheduled for tonight's bonfire please report to the mess hall."

Shane blew out his breath. "But you have to go," he finished.

"*We* have to go. Shane—"

Shane held up a finger to her lips. "No. It's cool. They need you."

Mitchie knew she was lucky to have such a supportive boyfriend. "Aren't you coming?"

"I'll catch up," he promised, walking toward the dock.

Mitchie watched him go—and then hurried off toward the mess hall.

It was a perfect summer night. Everyone at Camp Rock was outside, gathering around the huge bonfire. People were roasting marshmallows, strumming guitars, playing charades . . . a great end to a great day.

Jason was sitting alongside Mitchie's mom by the fire.

"I'm impressed," she told him as the Junior Rockers raced by, high-fiving him as they passed. "You seem to be doing much better with them."

Jason nodded. "Yeah, it took a little while, but I think I've finally earned their respect."

He stood up—but the log he had been sitting on was still attached to him. "Huh?" He bent over and tried to shake the log loose.

"All right," he grumbled as Trevor filmed him. "Who glued me to the log?"

The Junior Rockers were doubled over with

laughter. "Log Butt! Log Butt!" Gage taunted. "We're gonna call you Log Butt."

"Fine," Jason said, crossing his arms. "But you know the only thing worse than being called Log Butt? Being sat on by a Log Butt." And to the Junior Rockers delight, he ran after them.

"Look!" shouted a young camper. "Fireflies!" Sure enough, fireflies were flitting across the lawn near the water. The campers stood up and began to chase them. They didn't realize that across the lake, Axel Turner was watching the blissful chaos through his binoculars with Luke and Tess beside him.

"It's like *Lord of the Flies* over there," he muttered, handing the binoculars to Luke. "There's no way they're making it through the summer." Satisfied with what he'd seen, he walked away.

"I remember doing that," Tess said longingly, watching a group of laughing campers. "It's fun."

"Don't even think about it," Luke snapped.

But Tess couldn't help herself.

Back at Mitchie's cabin, Mitchie, Caitlyn, Peggy, Ella, Barron, and Sander were sitting outside on the porch, enjoying the summer-night breeze. Mitchie played a few chords on her guitar as her friends talked about the day's events.

"It felt so great just standing up in front of that class today," Peggy said, leaning against a pillar.

Caitlyn nodded. "I feel like there's nothing we can't do."

Ella groaned. "Pleats. Still can't do pleats."

Sander cracked his knuckles. "Wish we had that attitude the other night at Camp Star."

"Yeah," Barron agreed. "I so wanted to shove it right back in their faces."

Mitchie understood exactly how he'd felt. It had been so frustrating sitting there watching Luke strut across the stage with his fancy lights and backup dancers.

"That hardly counted," Peggy pointed out.

"They'd been planning that for weeks."

"Yeah, but now they're all walking around thinking they're better than us," Barron said angrily.

"*So* not true," Peggy said. "I'd like to see them really go up against us."

Caitlyn's eyes grew wide. "If we had the time to get it together, there is no way they'd even stand a chance. Like in Final Jam . . ."

"There is just no way," Peggy said.

"Camp Rock rules!" Sander shouted. "We're so much better."

"Lots of big talk," Mitchie chimed in, a mischievous smile on her lips. "Wanna see if it's true?"

CHAPTER 7

Mitchie had barely slept, thinking about her big plan to knock Camp Star off its pedestal. The next morning she gulped down her breakfast and met up with her friends. It was time to invade Camp Star.

"Let's do this," Mitchie told her friends, who were just as pumped up as she was. Mitchie, Caitlyn, Sander, Barron, and the rest of the campers had canoed over to Camp Star with their instruments in tow. Now they were marching toward the amphitheater. Drums were beating, hands were clapping, and the Camp Rockers were ready to show Camp Star what they were all about.

Stomping onto the main stage, Nate slid behind one of the drum sets and began to bang away.

"Yeah, we're here and on your stage," Mitchie said, grabbing a mike and addressing the Star campers that were flooding into the amphitheater. "Didn't really get a chance to answer back the other night. But that's about to change. Camp Rock versus Camp Star in Final Jam. What do you say? Think you can?" No takers. Mitchie grinned. "Yeah, that's what we thought."

Sure, Camp Star could pull out all the stops on a performance they'd rehearsed for weeks. But an impromptu jam session? Mitchie had had a feeling they couldn't begin to compete.

Jason and Shane plugged in their guitars and

began to play as Mitchie started to sing. She spotted Luke standing off to the side and stared directly at him as she sang. She'd show him just how good they were.

A few seconds later, Tess came sashaying across the stage, a posse of girls dancing and singing back-up behind her.

Mitchie couldn't deny it—Tess was good. After all, her mother was an award-winning singer, and Tess definitely had inherited those genes. Yet, Mitchie wasn't intimidated. She knew that she and her friends had a definite advantage. Not only were they just as talented—they were determined.

Pretty soon kids from both camps were singing, dancing, and playing their instruments, trying to one-up each other. It was musical mayhem—until Axel Turner came running up to the stage, getting between the two sides. "That is a fantastic idea," he said. "Truly, I'm impressed. A little healthy competition is exactly what we need."

Luke stared at him. "We do?"

"A champion always needs a good sparring partner," Axel replied.

Mitchie and her friends began to make some noise. No way was Luke worthy of being called a champion when he hadn't won a thing.

"You really think you can take on my guys head-to-head?" Axel asked the Camp Rockers.

Peggy stepped forward. "Anytime. Anyplace."

Axel shrugged and looked around him. "Maybe use our amphitheater?"

"It doesn't matter where," Mitchie said, hating how cocky he was. "Camp Rock is going to blow you away."

Axel gave Mitchie a haughty smirk. "I'm sure an audience would be a better judge of that."

"Bring it on!" Caitlyn challenged him. "You can pack it with anybody you want."

Axel rubbed his hands together, his eyes gleaming in the lights. "Then what about a worldwide audience? What if we put this little competition on TV and let the public decide who's really the best?"

Mitchie looked at her friends. She wasn't sure that was such a good idea. She didn't trust Axel, and if he was suggesting a televised competition, she could bet he'd stop at nothing to come out on top. But her friends looked really excited at the prospect.

"TV?" Ella kept repeating. "We'd really get to be on TV?"

"That would be so cool!" Peggy exclaimed, practically squealing.

"Uh, I don't know," Mitchie hedged, not wanting to commit to anything before they checked with Brown. Then she caught Luke's eye.

"Not such a big talker now, are you?" he said smugly.

"The whole world would see us," Caitlyn whispered, tugging Mitchie's arm.

That was the problem, Mitchie thought. They would have to be perfect. No way could they accept this invitation and come out anywhere but on top. Otherwise not only would their pride be stomped on . . . Camp Rock would be finished.

"Mitchie, come on," Sander begged. "This could be huge."

But if they didn't do this, Camp Rock could *still* be finished. She didn't have a choice.

"You're on," Mitchie finally told Axel, gritting her teeth in determination as finally everyone started cheering.

Back at Camp Rock in the mess hall, Mitchie and the other counselors sat at one of the tables. Her songwriting notebook was being passed from person to person. There was a song Mitchie had written that she felt pretty good about. And she hoped everyone else agreed with her.

"I think it could really work," Mitchie told them. "I wrote it last summer but I'd kind of forgotten about it."

"It's a duet," Nate pointed out.

Mitchie nodded. "Now. But I can rewrite it so there are parts for everybody." It would be a lot of work, but if they pulled it off it would be worth it.

"Or *we* could rewrite it," Shane offered, catching her eye.

Mitchie smiled at him. She loved collaborating on her music, especially with someone as talented as Shane. Together they could make this a song no one would ever forget.

Ella was looking at the notebook. "'I lay pretty, pretty flowers on your grave,'" she read aloud somberly. "Am I the only one who thinks this song is, like, totally depressing?"

Peggy leaned over to see where Ella was reading and frowned. "You're on the wrong page."

Mitchie tried not to laugh. "That was for my hamster's funeral."

Peggy and Barron were talking excitedly. "The staging could be pretty cool," Peggy said.

"And there's a ton of spots for some great dancing," Caitlyn added, tapping her pen on the table.

"We could do this kind of thing, where everybody's up there," Sander said, gesturing with his hands.

Mitchie could tell that her friends were just as into this as she was. And the great thing was they each brought a different perspective to the performance.

"You know, before we go any farther I just want to say that I've got some conditions," Jason spoke up.

Nate blinked. "You've got conditions?"

Jason backed up. "Okay, more like a condition. But it's nonnegotiable. There has to be a spot for my Junior Rockers."

"There will be a part for everyone," Mitchie told him. That's what their entire performance was meant to show the world—that Camp Rock brought out the best in everyone—not just a few star performers. She turned to Shane, who'd been drinking it all in. "So what do you think?"

"I think somebody needs to talk to Brown."

Mitchie grinned. "Why? I already know what he's going to say," she replied happily. Brown loved Camp Rock, and they were going to save it. It was a no-brainer.

Inside Brown's office the mood was a little different. Brown had just found out about Mitchie's plan. And he wasn't happy.

"How could they do that?" he exclaimed as Connie stood in the doorway. "I told them. I told Mitchie . . . Axel cannot be trusted!"

Connie studied him. "I don't know why you're so upset," she said. "At the very least Camp Rock will get some great exposure."

But Brown was too busy pacing back and forth to listen. "He took advantage is what he did. He saw an opportunity and went for it. An opportunity to destroy me once and for all."

"And I thought Mitchie could be dramatic," Connie said, only half joking.

With an angry grunt, Brown yanked his chair out and sat down at his desk.

"So call him up and say no," Connie suggested. "It's not that big of a deal."

Brown snorted. "Oh, we're well past big deal." He turned his computer screen around. There was the Camp Rock logo next to the Camp Star logo. Above them, an online newspaper heading read: CAMP WARS.

"'Camp Wars.' Catchy," Brown said, his voice dripping with sarcasm. "I especially like the tagline, 'Only one will survive.'"

Neither Connie nor Brown noticed that Mitchie had walked over to the screen door and was standing outside, listening. Mitchie had been about to walk in. But when she'd heard the serious tone of her mother's voice, she'd halted outside to eavesdrop.

"We'll be watched by millions of people," Connie said, trying to muster up some enthusiasm in the camp director. "That's good, right?"

"After this—we're done," Brown said, shaking

his head. "And not just for the summer . . . for good."

Mitchie sucked in her breath. This was not the reaction she'd anticipated when she'd come up with her plan. Brown wasn't happy with her—he was upset.

"Give them a chance," Connie urged, putting her palms on the desk.

"Nobody believes in my rockers more than I do, but we are going to look like a joke next to Camp Star," Brown told her ruefully. "We don't have the resources. The money. The infrastructure." He took a deep breath. "Talent, passion, commitment—it's not going to matter."

"It always matters," Connie said quietly.

"And when people watch," Brown went on, "where do you think they're going to send their kids to camp?"

Mitchie felt like she couldn't breathe. All she'd wanted to do was help—but Brown was furious with her!

"She didn't do it on purpose," Connie told him.

"I know," Brown said, rubbing tiredly at his temples. "She was just trying to help. I'm not mad at her. I just wish she hadn't—"

Mitchie couldn't stand it any longer. She turned and fled down the old wooden steps, tears flooding her brown eyes.

She had wanted to do the right thing—help Brown save Camp Rock. Now, everything was a big mess and it was all her fault. She'd never in a million years wanted to let anyone down, especially not Camp Rock. This place, these people—it was like her second family.

A sob catching in her throat, she walked toward the beach. She'd have to try and turn it all around. Figure out how to fix things.

Before it was too late.

CHAPTER 8

The sound of a hammer pounding a new schedule onto the board rang out across Camp Rock the next morning. Then Sander's voice came over the PA system.

"Good morning, Camp Rock. All Rockers report to the main stage immediately. Yeah, that means you. Get movin'!"

Once everyone had assembled, Mitchie greeted them. She had a huge megaphone in her hands that she used to speak to the crowd. "All right, Rockers, there are new schedules up on the boards. From this moment on, everything is about winning the competition. Everything. We have to be completely focused."

"What about swimming and waterskiing?" Barron called out from the crowd as several kids around him nodded.

"Focused!" Mitchie cried. Then she winced as Barron covered his ears. "Sorry." Oops. She probably shouldn't have used the megaphone, considering she was standing only two feet away from him.

She put the megaphone down. "Sorry, again. Seriously, if we want to save the camp, we have to put all of our energies into this and make it the best show any of us have ever done." She saw that Brown had walked over and was standing on the edge of the crowd. She hadn't spoken to him since listening in on his conversation with her mother. But there wasn't anything to say, except . . . "We may have our doubters, but we've already come so far—we can't go down now. Agreed?" she asked.

"Agreed!" they yelled back in unison.

"Okay." Mitchie gave them an encouraging smile. "Then let's get to work."

No one moved. Mitchie picked up the megaphone and shouted into it, "Now!"

That did the trick.

Inside Brown's office, Mitchie had spread out schedules, lists, and pages of ideas. The place resembled a well-organized war room. She pointed to one of the plans.

"I don't know what to do about the set, but it's just got to be big," she said to a couple of guys who were helping her strategize. "Think of the biggest thing you can imagine . . . then make it bigger."

"Knock, knock," came Shane's voice from outside. He opened the screen door and came in holding up one of the new schedules. "Uh, we seem to be moving in the wrong direction," he said, tossing it on the table. "There's even less free time on this than the old one."

That was true, but there weren't really other options. Mitchie glanced at the clock. "I've got a few minutes now."

Shane grimaced. "Not really what I was thinking, but—"

Just then Ella came flying into the office. "Mitchie. Can you look at this?" she asked breathlessly, waving fabric swatches and sketches in front of Mitchie's face. "I want us to coordinate but not be all matchy-matchy."

Caitlyn was two steps behind her. "Mitchie— hey, Shane—I know you're rewriting, but we've got to make some decisions about the music."

Sander and Peggy followed. They too had ideas they wanted to run by Mitchie.

"Hey, Mitch," Shane interjected, looking a little put out. "Can I have you for a sec?"

"Do you know who's doing the vocal arrangements?" Peggy wanted to know, ignoring

Shane. "If it's me, fine—but someone's got to tell me."

Mitchie bit her lip. "Sorry," she mouthed to Shane. There just weren't enough hours in the day to get everything she wanted accomplished done. And right now, focusing on Camp Rock was where her head needed to be.

Shane stood there for a moment as if he was about to say something. Then, giving up, he walked outside, letting the screen door bang behind him. Mitchie looked up for a second—and then Caitlyn was asking her something about the sound mixing. Mitchie couldn't let herself think about Shane.

This was just too important to mess up.

Nate had finally met a girl he was interested in getting to know—and they might as well have been an ocean apart. Or, well, a lake.

He dragged his foot through the sand, squinting in the sunlight across the water. He loved being at Camp Rock . . . but it would have been nice to have a girl to keep him company.

Just then Shane came walking—or rather, stalking—past. "I swear I don't even know why I'm here," Shane muttered, not slowing down. "Take my advice. Never, ever get yourself a girlfriend."

Nate sighed. "No worries about that." He held up his binoculars and looked across the lake to Camp Star. Dana was standing on the dock, holding her own pair of binoculars. He gave a little wave, and she waved back. Nate put his binoculars down and sadly headed back toward camp.

"**H**ey, hey, what are you doing?" Mitchie scolded as she walked past her cabin. Caitlyn and a couple of her dance students were there, but instead of practicing their routine, they were laughing and goofing around. "You guys are supposed to be rehearsing," Mitchie reminded them.

Caitlyn laughed. "Calm down. We've been rehearsing for over five hours. We're just taking a little break." She did an exaggerated slide across the floor.

But Mitchie wasn't in the mood for fun and games. "Yeah, well, I was watching, and I think we're going to need a lot more work," she said tartly before walking over to Peggy. She stood there, silent, as Peggy and another camper were busy cracking each other up.

"You guys done already?" Mitchie asked them.

Still laughing, Peggy said, "No. He was just telling this story about his sister. It's hilarious. You have to tell her," she said to him.

"Oh, is it the one about the group of kids who didn't take their jobs seriously and their camp was closed down? I've heard it," Mitchie snapped, watching Peggy's face fall. She couldn't believe her friends were being so cavalier about this.

She was stomping off when Jason came

running up to her with Trevor and a few other Junior Rockers behind him.

"Mitchie," Jason said, out of breath, "you've got to see this bit me and the Junior Rockers came up with. I think it's a real spotlight moment."

"That's great, but whatever it is, it's probably going to be more of a background moment," she said, sidestepping him and making a beeline for Sander and his crew. "Sander! What's going on?" she called out. They were studying set plans—which was what they were doing when she'd left them a half hour ago. "We have to get this built! Come on guys, work with me."

She was dismayed to hear Sander mutter under his breath, "If I wanted to go to Camp Star, I would have signed up."

She shook her head at him, frustrated. "That's not fair. I am just trying to get this done. But if you don't care . . ." she trailed off, feeling tears welling up in her eyes. Everyone was staring at her.

"Mitchie, we all care," Caitlyn told her. "But you've got to lighten up."

Mitchie swallowed back the lump that had formed in her throat. "Yeah, and what will that get us?"

Caitlyn stared at her for another moment, then turned back to her dancers. "All right, let's do it again."

Mitchie didn't care if everyone thought she was being mean. She wasn't trying to make friends. She was trying to save Camp Rock— her camp. Their camp. Couldn't they see that?

"That girl is taking the *f-u-n* out of *summer*," Ella said under her breath as Mitchie walked away.

"There is no *f-u-n* in *summer*," Peggy told her.

"Exactly," said Ella.

Brown and Shane had witnessed Mitchie's mini-meltdown. Now Peggy turned to them, hands on her hips. "Seriously, I love her, but I'm going to kill her."

"You know what you've got to do," Brown told his nephew.

Shane nodded, a gleam in his eye. "I'm on it."

As Shane headed toward the Junior Rockers' rec room, Jason was trying to convince his campers that Mitchie hadn't turned down his proposal— she'd said she'd think about it. But his pitch was cut short when Shane showed up.

"I've got a proposition for you boys," Shane said. "Think you're up for it?" Once they'd heard Shane's plan, they couldn't wait to put it into action.

All of the Camp Rockers were assembled in front of the stage, and Mitchie was speaking into her megaphone. "Okay, we have a ton of stuff to go over. Where are the Junior Rockers? And Shane? And Jason? And Nate? Seriously, people have got to start being on time. First off—"

"Attack!" Jason yelled, giving the signal.

The Junior Rockers invaded from all directions, whooping like warriors. Using homemade catapults, they launched water balloons into the air while Shane and Nate hopped onto the stage and began shooting people with water guns.

Mitchie looked aghast. "What do you think you're—*aaaah!*" Water blasted her from every side. The camp erupted into delighted shrieks and screams as all the campers got in on the fun, soakers and soakees alike.

"I don't think this was on the schedule," Connie told Brown, wringing her hands.

Brown grinned back. "Are you kidding? This is what summer camp is all about." He stepped forward. "Counterattack!" He whipped out a garden hose he'd kept hidden from view and blasted Jason. Then Brown began tossing out packets of balloons to various campers.

Delighted, the campers filled up their balloons at the spigot and reloaded the water guns down at the lake.

A water fight may not have been on the schedule. But it sure was fun.

* * *

Mitchie scribbled furiously in her songwriting notebook, stopped, groaned, and erased. She'd been sitting alone at a mess-hall table for hours, poring over each stanza and every melody. It had to be perfect.

"You know, your sheet music is soggy," Shane said as he walked inside. The screen door banged behind him.

"I'm pouring myself into the music," Mitchie joked. It was true, though. She hadn't even bothered to change her clothes after the water fight. She'd been so anxious to sit down and work on her lyrics, but they weren't flowing as easily as she needed them to.

Shane laughed at her joke. Then he said, "That was bad."

"I know." Mitchie winced, sliding over to make room for Shane alongside her. "Are you here to help?"

He shook his head. "I can't."

"Why not?" Mitchie asked.

Shane pulled her to her feet with one hand. "Because you and I are going on a moonlight picnic on the dock." In his other hand were a flashlight and a picnic basket. "Admittedly, all stolen from the mess-hall kitchen. Don't tell your mom."

Mitchie laughed. "Now?" He couldn't be serious. The timing . . .

"Right now."

"How could you—" Mitchie started to say at the same time as Shane said, "Because I really am just that nice of a guy."

Mitchie continued, "—think that I would just go running off?" It wasn't as if she could turn off a switch and pretend like she didn't have the weight of the world on her shoulders.

"Are you saying no?" Shane asked, his brown eyes disappointed.

Mitchie exhaled. "Do you not understand everything that needs to get done?"

"How could I not since I have you reminding me, like, every two seconds?" he said.

"And a water fight?" Mitchie scolded. "What were you thinking?"

Shane was frowning. "I was thinking, 'Wow, wouldn't it be nice to have fun for a change.'"

That stung. "So you're saying I'm not fun," Mitchie replied. It came out as more of a statement than a question.

Shane groaned. "I don't even know why I keep trying. The only reason I'm here—"

"Is to get to know me better," Mitchie finished for him, frustrated by the whole conversation. "I know. Well, guess what? This is me, and I'm trying to save something important to me."

Shane gave her a steady look. "Well, so am I."

"How's it working out for you?" Mitchie asked, hating how snippy she sounded but feeling powerless to stop herself.

"Not so good." He turned to go.

"Shane, wait!" Mitchie called after him. He turned back. "You forgot your flashlight."

Without a word, he took it and walked out.

Mitchie went back to her notebook, but

nothing she wrote was any good. She squeezed her eyes shut. She knew she'd been rude to Shane, but how could she just go hang out with him when so much was at stake? Why couldn't they see eye to eye on this?

Even though it seemed as if they were from different planets, Mitchie wouldn't change a thing about Shane. Sure, he could drive her crazy. But that didn't mean she wasn't crazy about him.

CHAPTER 9

Mitchie was in the middle of a horrible dream—she forgot the words to one of her songs in front of conceited Luke Williams—when a warm beam of sunlight splashed across her face, waking her up.

She rolled over, pulling her soft sheet close, then bolted up. She was alone in the cabin. The other beds were made, and the girls were gone. What time was it? And where were her friends?

She hopped out of bed, put on a pair of shorts, a staff T-shirt, and grabbed a hoodie. Slipping her flip-flops on, she padded outside.

The porch, the path, the lake . . . empty. A flock of birds flew overhead as Mitchie looked around.

She headed up to the main stage area. Here they are, she thought, hardly able to believe what she was seeing. Peggy was rehearsing singers. Caitlyn, Sander, and Barron were working out a dance routine. Jason was practicing guitar parts with the Junior Rockers. Ella was zipping around with her measuring tape, taking measurements for costumes. Another group was poring over set and lighting plans.

"What's going on?" Mitchie said, dumbfounded. This was the kind of effort she'd been trying to achieve all week long.

"You were right," Ella told her. "It shouldn't be all up to you. And we do need to step it up."

"But, how—?"

Caitlyn hopped down off the stage. "Shane

got everybody up before dawn," she explained, tugging on the hem of her tee. "He can be pretty persuasive when he wants to be."

A wave of gratitude—then guilt—swept over Mitchie. She looked around, spotting Shane with a group of other musicians.

"Mornin'," he told her, handing her some papers. "Sleep well? Here, I don't think you've seen a copy of the new arrangement yet. That song really needed a lot of work."

Mitchie looked at the papers in her hands, trying to process. "Did you do this?"

"Yup. I hope you like," Shane said with a smile.

Mitchie met his gaze, her heart thumping. "I already know I love it."

Later that afternoon, Mitchie and Shane were watching Caitlyn and a few other campers practicing a dance routine on the stage. They were pretty good, Mitchie thought, but something was missing. . . .

"No," Shane said, hopping up on the stage

and shaking his head. "You gotta work that stage like you own it." He grabbed a mike and did a classic pop-star strut, looking directly into a pretend camera with a confident glare.

He's such a natural, Mitchie marveled. That's what had been missing from their show—stage presence. That sure-of-yourself attitude that all successful performers needed.

"And guys," Shane called over to some campers on drums, "you're playing, but we gotta *see* you play. Nate?"

Nate hurried over with a couple of drumsticks. "Not like this," he told the drummers, playing the set quietly. "Like this." And he whaled on the drums, making a show of it.

"Jason," Shane said, motioning for his brother to step forward. "Show 'em how it's done."

Jason nodded. "Not like this," he said, lamely playing air guitar with zero energy. He waved his Junior Rockers over and they swarmed around him. "Guys?" he prompted. "Like this!" And they all broke out into some total instrument thrashing and killer rock-star poses.

"Woo-hoo!" Mitchie yelled appreciatively. The practice sessions with Jason had brought out their inner rock stars!

Caitlyn, however, wasn't so thrilled. "Well, that's easy for you guys, but we're not all rock stars," she told Shane.

"But you can be," Shane insisted, pumping his fist and grabbing an imaginary mike stand.

Being a rocker was so much more than just hitting the notes or knowing where your cue was, Mitchie had discovered. Playing a song perfectly was nice, but if you couldn't own the stage or put all your heart and soul into a performance, the audience wouldn't stay with you.

That was what rock and roll was all about.

And Mitchie loved every second of it.

A little while later, Nate walked along the path that led to his cabin, humming a song that he just couldn't get out of his head. Then he struck a pose and pretended he was onstage, rocking out. Check it out, he thought, jumping onto a bench and leaning back as if he was playing an incredible solo.

"Hi, Nate."

Nate spun around so fast that he lost his balance and toppled over into a nearby bush. He would have never acted like such a goofball if he'd known someone was there. Such as Dana!

"Dana. Hi," Nate said, covering. "I didn't. . . . What are you doing here?" he blurted out, scrambling to his feet.

"What do you think?" she asked him.

"You came to see me?" Nate tried, hoping that was the case.

She smiled. "Good guess."

"Well . . . here I am," Nate told her, spreading his arms wide. But his words didn't exactly elicit the reaction he was expecting.

Dana stared at him, an annoyed expression on her face. "That's it? I came all the way over here in a canoe, risking my father's wrath, and that's all you have to say to me?" she exclaimed.

Nate gulped. "I don't know what else I'm supposed to say," he said. His palms were beginning to sweat.

"There's nothing you're *supposed* to say," Dana retorted, her eyes flashing. "Every day I see you looking and waving, and I'm all, *that's so sweet, I so like him.*"

"You do?" Nate said. She did like him! "That's really what you say?"

"But then . . ." she began, shaking her head.

"But then," Nate repeated, feeling like a balloon that had lost its air. "That's never good."

"How can I really know if I don't know anything about you?" She folded her arms across her chest. "I guess I thought you were different."

Nate had to say something to turn this conversation around. "I am different," he said. "My brothers tell me that all the time."

Now Dana looked angry. "No, you're not. You're exactly like every other sixteen-year-old boy in the world." She made her voice sound dorky. "Uh, I don't know," she mimicked. "Have you ever asked me a question or told me anything about yourself—you know, other than you like canoeing?" she demanded to know. "What's you favorite holiday? Do you like to read? Waffles or pancakes? Are you afraid of the dark?" She took a deep, ragged breath. "And it's Thanksgiving, yes, neither, and no, in case you're interested," she added, answering her own questions.

No one had ever spoken like that to Nate before. He blinked. "I don't really like canoeing," he confessed, shrugging. There, that was something. Right?

"So I really know nothing about you," Dana said, frowning.

A long awkward moment of silence hung in the air.

"I still don't know what to say," Nate mumbled, shoving his hands in his pockets. When he was onstage he felt so self-assured, but when he was face-to-face with a girl he really liked? Hello insecurity.

"It's okay," Dana replied. "I think you just did." And she brushed past him and headed down the path.

"Idiot," Nate muttered, shaking his head. But he didn't stop her.

The next day, Mitchie couldn't keep the smile off her face when she saw Shane coming down the hill toward the lake. She had the boat ready to go, and soon they were rowing across the water.

"Are you sure you have the time?" Shane asked, half serious. His foot jostled a picnic basket packed with goodies.

Mitchie nodded. "You make time for what's important," she replied, smiling. After watching Shane and his brothers inspire the campers with their passion for music, she'd taken a step back from things for a moment. Although saving Camp Rock was at the very top of her list, there was room for something else at the top, too.

Someone else—Shane. So this morning she'd given her mom a note to pass along to him when he stood in the breakfast line.

Meet me at the
lake at 11.
I miss you.
          -Mitchie.
p.s. I've got
   lunch covered.

The rest of the afternoon was just about as perfect as it could be. Shane wasn't the best oarsman—they crashed into a cluster of rocks not once, but twice—and then he'd actually lost his paddle.

But that was okay. Mitchie couldn't think of anyone else she'd rather hang out with and talk to—or eat her mom's egg salad and pickle sandwiches with. And when they were together, it was okay not to talk, too. They spent a half hour floating quietly along the lake, the only sound an occasional splash as birds dove for fish.

Mitchie let out a contented sigh as she sat next to Shane with her legs dangling in the water. If there was a better way to spend a summer afternoon, she didn't know it.

Later that afternoon, Nate was enjoying a good old-fashioned mopefest in his cabin when Shane came walking by, a lovesick grin on his face. "I take back what I said about girlfriends," Shane said, poking his head in the cabin window next to Nate.

"Too bad, because at this rate I'll never have one," Nate grumbled.

Shane's eyebrows shot up. "What's going on?" he asked.

"I'm an idiot," Nate declared. "You can agree."

Shane hesitated. "You're not going to hit me?"

"No."

"Then I totally agree," Shane said, smiling.

Nate was too depressed to even react. "There's this girl," he started.

"I kinda figured," Shane said.

"I really like her, but I'm having trouble telling her how I feel," Nate admitted.

Suddenly Jason's head popped into view through another cabin window. "Dude, you're a rock star. Use it."

Nate let out a frustrated groan. "I don't think she cares. She wants to know all of this stupid random stuff about me," he explained.

"Not random stuff," Shane corrected him. "She wants to know you care enough to let her know who you really are."

Nate let that sink in for a moment. It made sense. "But what if I don't know?" he asked miserably.

The more Nate thought about what Shane had said, the more Nate knew he had to do something. So he paddled over to Camp Star and hid behind a cluster of trees, waiting for Dana to appear. When Axel, Tess, and Luke came out of the main building, Nate couldn't help but overhear their conversation.

"I just think if I was more center stage for the second verse . . ." Tess was saying, hurrying after Axel.

"Every single time I finish the note, I'm behind her big head!" Luke was yelling.

"Enough!" Axel cut off their bickering. He turned to the stage manager. "We're going to run it again in three minutes. And this time, let's try and remember that it's not amateur hour!"

"He means you," Tess grumbled to Luke, flipping her hair over her shoulder.

Just then Dana came out of the building. Nate jogged forward. "Hi, Dana."

She spun around, looking surprised to see him.

"Kind of makes you jump, doesn't it?" he said, forcing a laugh to try and lighten the mood.

Dana wasn't smiling. "You shouldn't be here."

"I know, but I couldn't wait," Nate told her, straightening his shoulders.

"Wait for what?" she asked.

He handed her a wrinkled sheet of notebook paper on which he'd written a list. A really long list. "It's a list of things nobody knows about me," he said, feeling better about himself than he had in a long time.

"Two minutes!" the stage manager called out.

Dana looked torn. "I really gotta go. I'm sorry." As she turned to go back to the main stage, Nate reached for her arm. "Wait! You still have two minutes."

Since he had been having so much trouble talking about his feelings, he'd decided to express them the best way he knew how—through a song. Nate picked up the guitar he'd brought and began to sing. It was a song he'd written for Dana—about himself. He called it "Introducing Me." Instead of a lot of empty words about love, he'd worked hard to write a song that would have real meaning for her.

He felt kind of embarrassed, at first, singing about liking cheese only when it was on pizza and confessing that he was trying to grow a mustache. But if she wanted to know about him, he was going to show her the real him—not the cool pop star that shined onstage but the person behind all that.

And so he sang about loving old guitars, superheroes, the sound of violins, and making someone smile. If he was going to let Dana into his world, he wanted to show her everything. He wanted to let her know what he thought and how he felt.

It may have been more than she ever wanted to know, but he was done trying to impress her by acting cool.

As he finished, he saw her face burst into the biggest smile he'd ever seen.

And Nate was grinning right back. He'd done it! But before he could say anything, he heard the sharp, angry voice of her father.

"Dana!" If Axel Turner had been a cartoon

character, smoke would have been pouring from his ears. He stood there, fuming. "Everyone's waiting."

"It was my fault," Nate said, swallowing.

"Why don't you save the theatrics for the competition," Axel told him. "We'll talk about this later," he said to Dana.

"It's okay. Go. And, Nate?" She reached over and took the piece of notebook paper. "Thank you." As she hurried away with her father, Nate pumped his fist.

Who knew telling a girl you only liked cheese when it was on pizza could feel so awesome?

CHAPTER 10

"**A**nd all that was left was a bloody footprint," Gage, the Junior Rocker, was saying, holding a flashlight up under his chin. It was nighttime, and he and the other Junior Rockers were sitting in a dark cabin with Jason, telling ghost stories.

The boys all looked at one another, shadows flickering over their faces.

"Lame," Trevor said.

"Not even scary," scoffed a boy named Jamal.

Jason gulped. Were these kids crazy? That was one of the freakiest things he'd ever heard. He cleared his throat. "So lame. Okay, let's put the lights on and get into bed."

Gage looked at him. "But you called lights-out."

"Lights-out?" Jason scoffed, shaking out his sleeping bag. "Who would ever want to sleep with the lights out?" He flopped down on his bunk, and the boys followed suit.

Snap. Jason bolted up when he heard a stick crack outside. Was it a bear? A lost camper? A serial killer with a bloody footprint? "Did anybody hear that?" No one said anything. Apparently not. He lay back down, his pulse racing.

"Jason, do you think we're gonna win?" Jamal asked, his voice sounding small in the dark.

"Totally. You're rock stars," Jason told him.

"But what if they are, too?" Jamal wanted to know.

Jason considered this. "I don't know. I hadn't

thought that far." He lay there, mulling it over. Then he had an idea. He sat up again. They'd need to grab their sweatshirts, shoes, bug spray . . . and flashlights.

There was definitely no sneaking out without flashlights.

A little while later, Jason and his Junior Rockers were zipping in and out of the bushes and trees that dotted the Camp Star landscape, trying to stay unnoticed. They were hoping to spy on the opposing camp's rehearsal, but their plan would fail if they were discovered.

"Stay low," Jason instructed, his voice barely audible. He ducked out of the underbrush and raced to the next group of shrubs. The Junior Rockers, with branches taped to the tops of their Camp Rock baseball caps, followed. As they reached the top of a leafy slope, Jason leaped over the edge.

"Roll. Roll," he called as he slid down the hill. Then, as sticks and rocks jabbed his skin, he rethought that. "Ow! Ow! Rocks. Don't roll. Don't roll!" He got to his feet. "Climb down carefully," he told the Junior Rockers, who began to tentatively make their way down.

"That's it," Jason whispered, encouraging them. "Watch your step."

In the short time they'd been together, they had come a long way. He was very proud of them.

They reached the top of a small wall that gave them a perfect view of the Camp Star amphitheater. Even though it was past most people's bedtime, there was major activity going on there. A crew was hard at work building a glittery set. Axel Turner was onstage barking directions. Jason spotted Luke and Tess, along with some other Star campers going through what appeared to be a rehearsal. Then, the entire stage was lit up by lasers, and Luke and Tess began to sing. They looked and sounded amazing.

Trevor pulled out his video camera, trained

it on the stage, and hit RECORD.

Moments later, it was time to head back.

They needed to tell the Camp Rockers what they had seen!

𝒯he next morning, Mitchie and the other counselors gathered around Jason and an excited group of Junior Rockers at the mess hall to watch Trevor's Camp Star video.

"They have this cannon thing," Trevor was explaining as footage played of a glitter-shooting cannon. "And the stage is supercool."

"It was huge," said Erin, another one of the Junior Rockers.

Shane's eyes were glued to the screen. "Wait. Slow down. So it's just Tess and that Luke guy singing?" he asked. "Really?"

Jason nodded. "Yeah. Pretty much everyone else is doing something, but they're definitely the stars."

Caitlyn let out a snort. "I can't believe Tess's head will even fit on the stage."

"Are you sure?" Shane asked Jason.

"We watched it, like, ten times," Jason told him.

"Yeah, you think Mitchie's mean, you should see that Tess girl," Erin muttered to a few of the counselors.

"Hey!" Mitchie cried, giving Erin a fake punch.

"But this makes it so much easier," Peggy spoke up. "We can totally win this now."

Mitchie was confused. "How so?"

Ella sighed. "Oh, come on, even I get it. I don't care what they're singing, but you and Shane are better than Tess and Luke any day."

Everyone nodded.

"But Shane and I aren't singing together," Mitchie reminded them.

"But you originally wrote the song as a duet," Caitlyn reminded her back, raising an eyebrow.

Mitchie balked. "I know, but—"

"I'm normally not the kind of girl who likes to sing backup, but I'd totally do it for you two," Peggy volunteered.

"We'll tone down some of the moves, pull the guys back a little," Sander said, thinking out loud.

Barron agreed. "You're our two strongest singers."

Caitlyn's eyes were twinkling. "And we know you've got chemistry."

Mitchie really appreciated this amazing vote of confidence. But it didn't really seem fair. "Everybody worked so hard," she protested. This wasn't the Mitchie and Shane show—it was about *all* of Camp Rock.

"To help save the camp," Caitlyn said firmly. "If the two of you singing lead could help us win, then we have to do this."

Mitchie felt incredibly torn. Uncertain, she turned to Shane. "What do you think?"

He shrugged. "Sounds like we don't have a choice."

"Then it's settled," Peggy said firmly. The counselors and the Junior Rockers all started talking at once about how to change the show.

Out of the corner of her eye, Mitchie noticed that Trevor, Jamal, and a couple other Junior Rockers were slinking out of the mess hall, small shoulders slumped. She walked over to them.

"You guys okay?" she asked, concerned.

"Yeah," Jamal said, sounding dejected. "I was just looking forward to doing some of my new moves."

"But it's okay," Trevor added quickly. "You know, if it means we get to come back here next summer." He held up his video camera and looked at the images on the screen, smiling.

"You had a good summer?" Mitchie asked, hating how sad the Junior Rockers were.

Trevor nodded. "Only, like, the best summer ever."

She looked down at his screen as a video clip of Trevor and the Junior Rockers chasing after Jason played. Then, a lightbulb went off in her head. She put her arms around the boys and gave them a squeeze, kissing each of their heads.

"Ew, gross!" Trevor cried.

"Get off of me!" Jamal protested, wiping off her kiss.

Mitchie laughed, then ran back toward the counselors in the mess hall. "Guys!" she screamed. "I've got a great idea!" And if it worked, not only would she save Camp Rock . . . they *all* would.

CHAPTER 11

After weeks of preparation and anticipation, the big moment finally arrived. The Camp Star amphitheater was filling up, and TV cameras were positioned on the stage. A huge lighted sign that read HITZ TV hung above it.

A TV host fixed her earpiece and faced the camera. "Hello and welcome to Hitz TV. I'm Georgina Farlow, and today we're bringing you 'Camp Wars'—the ultimate summer-camp showdown. There can only be one winner in this Final Jam, and your votes are going to help us decide. Just call or text in after each performance—kids, make sure to get your parents' permission—and let us know who you think sang out and who you think hit the wrong note. What's *your* favorite camp—Camp Star or Camp Rock?"

When the introduction spot was finished, the TV host walked over to Axel and Brown.

"Great to see you, Georgina," Axel said, shaking her hand.

She gave a curt, professional nod. "As always, Axel. I'm going to go do some stand-ups backstage before the concert. Good luck." And she walked away.

"You know her?" Brown asked, surprised.

"I know everybody," Axel said smoothly. "But don't worry, she doesn't have anything to do with the voting."

Brown hadn't been thinking about that, but now he wondered—had Axel somehow fixed the show's results? He wished things could be different with his former friend and bandmate. But he knew they never would. "So I probably shouldn't hold out hope for us ever being friends again," he said.

"Probably not," Axel replied, sounding upbeat. "Though you never know. Next year I might need to hire you to run my summer camp."

Brown smirked. "Thanks, but I'm already booked."

Mitchie was filled with anxiety as she stood in the wings of the Camp Star amphitheater, getting ready for the final showdown. She'd just witnessed Luke and Tess having a backstage spat—but Tess being Tess, she covered it up by plastering a big smile on her face.

The stage manager motioned for everyone to get in their places, and Georgina Farlow walked onstage to wild applause. With spotlights shining down on her, Georgina began to speak in a dramatic voice. "As the sun goes down, the volume goes up. Welcome back to the ultimate summer-camp showdown, where *you* decide the winner. First up is Camp Star. Camp Star was founded only this year by superstar producer and founder of Star Records, Axel Turner, who's been producing hits for over twenty years. I know if I was going to study music, this is the place I'd want to be."

Caitlyn nudged Mitchie. "Why is she saying that?" she hissed.

"It's her job," Mitchie whispered back. "She's supposed to say nice things."

Ella's face was pale. "If she doesn't stop talking, I think I'm going to throw up." She grimaced. "Too late." She ran off to find a bathroom.

Mitchie could sympathize—the entire experience was so nerve-racking it was enough to make the very best performers sick. She watched as Georgina introduced Camp Star.

As Mitchie expected, the Camp Star set was amazing, complete with a multileveled stage, catwalks, and intricate backdrops. And also as expected, Luke and Tess were the stars of the show while the rest of the Star campers did perfectly synchronized backup dance moves, singing flawlessly.

Except Mitchie hadn't expected them to sound quite *as* good . . . or dance *as* amazingly as they did . . . or have *such* detailed, elaborate costumes.

The lyrics were completely over-the-top. Luke and Tess sang about how they had the confidence to command the stage, own the crowd, and steal the show. They are literally singing their own praises, Mitchie thought. She exchanged a worried glance with Shane as dancers ran on and off the stage. As much as she hated to admit it, their performance was great. Really great.

And the crowd knew it. As the Camp Star performers finished, the audience was on their feet, cheering and clapping.

"I kind of wish I hadn't watched," Peggy said,

expressing the thoughts of all the Camp Rock counselors.

"Me, too," Caitlyn muttered. "I hate it when Tess is good."

Now Mitchie was the one who felt sick to her stomach as Luke and Tess took their bows. But we're great, too, she reminded herself, clapping politely. And when Luke and Tess exited the stage, she gave them a sincere smile. "Congratulations! You guys were really good."

"I know, right?" Luke boasted, full of himself as always. "Only one thing would have made it better," he said, sauntering off. "Doing it solo."

"For once I totally agree!" Tess yelled after him, scowling. She turned to Mitchie, all smiles. "It's this little bantery thing we . . . Thanks. That means a lot."

Having to perform with Luke had to be pretty brutal for someone like Tess. Mitchie didn't blame her for trying to act as if things were perfect between them.

But there was no time to feel even a teeny

bit bad for Tess Tyler. Mitchie had to steady her nerves and focus on her own performance.

"Weren't they incredible?" Georgina Farlow was back onstage. "Camp Star, everyone. Remember, if you loved them as much as I did, call or text in now. But don't go away, because in a few moments we're gonna hear from Camp Rock!"

The Camp Rockers were all standing there, gazing out at the stage, full of opening-night nerves. Mitchie clapped. "That's us! Everybody move." Startled into action, the campers dashed to their places.

Shane ran over. "Have you seen Nate?"

Mitchie shook her head, looking around.

While Shane was wondering about his brother's whereabouts, Nate was over by the keyboard section, trying to get to Dana before she left. He whipped out a bouquet of flowers he'd brought with him from Camp Rock. "I thought you were a star," he told her, handing her the flowers.

Dana gave him a smile. "Thanks."

"I really gotta go," Nate told her, walking away—and then running back. "Oh, and I hate crust on my bread, and birds make me nervous." Once that was off his chest he turned to go and found himself face-to-face with Dana's dad. Again.

"Sorry, but once you start expressing your innermost thoughts and desires, it's hard to stop," Nate blurted out. Then he called back to Dana one last time. "Wish me luck!"

"Good luck!" she cried, tossing him her DANA bracelet. With a huge grin, he caught it and took off running.

"Dana! He's the enemy," her father reprimanded her.

"No, he's not," Dana said, standing up to her father. "Everything in life is not a competition." Then she lifted the bouquet to her nose and inhaled its sweet scent. "But I think I just won."

"**A**nd we're back," Georgina announced dramatically from the Camp Star stage. She looked out at the crowd. "If you liked Camp Star, well, get ready to be blown away by Camp Rock!"

Mitchie stood next to Shane in the wings. She'd just received a text telling her to vote for Camp Star. Clearly, Axel was using his connections to try to influence the results. But there was no time to worry about it now. Shane's eyes were fixed on hers.

"Ready?" he asked, squeezing her hand.

"Ready! Let's show them what Camp Rock is all about," Mitchie replied.

Georgina's voice boomed through her mike: "Ladies and gentlemen, Camp Rock!"

The Camp Rock opening was a lot like Camp Star's. Mitchie and Shane began singing under a spotlight, just as Tess and Luke had a short while ago. Except a few moments into their song, lights began to come up across the stage, and soon *all* the Camp Rockers were coming out to perform—singing, playing guitars, dancing.

Then, as Mitchie sang, she saw her great idea

come to life. On one of Camp Star's huge flat screens, Trevor's video footage of the summer began to play.

There was Jason with the Junior Rockers, trying to fish Trevor's camera out of the lake; Mitchie singing to a clearly smitten Shane in the Camp Star amphitheater; Barron and Sander rocking out in the DJ booth; Jason chasing the Junior Rockers around the rec room; Nate teaching drums to the campers; Caitlyn showing a room full of dancers some incredible moves; Ella dressing up a camper in an original Ella design; the Junior Rockers giving Jason a present: a rock-and-roll birdhouse; Mitchie playing the piano as her friends gather around, singing; Shane playing Frisbee with some campers on the beach; Connect 3 performing; Mitchie and Shane on a rowboat; campers catching fireflies, roasting marshmallows, splashing in the lake, drinking "bug juice."

Mitchie poured her heart into the song, a song that captured everything she felt about this magical, amazing summer with her awesome friends. And there was the proof up on the screen—proof that it had been a wonderful summer for *everyone* at Camp Rock.

As the music ended, the packed theater erupted into thunderous applause. They loved us! Mitchie thought excitedly, sneaking a peek at Shane. They'd put everything they had into this performance.

Hopefully it would be enough.

"**W**ow, now that really was incredible!" Georgina enthused as the Camp Rockers joined hands for an ensemble bow. "So call in now and let us know which summer camp rules! Stay tuned, we'll be right back."

"And we're out," said the stage manager.

Sander bounced from person to person. "Call in! Call in!"

Everyone scrambled for their phones and madly started texting.

"All right, everybody to their places, we're

back in thirty seconds!" the stage manager barked.

When it was time for the results, Mitchie felt like everything was moving in slow motion. She and the other Camp Rockers stood on one side. The Star campers were on the opposite side. Shane held Mitchie's hand, and she closed her eyes as the lights flashed on and they were back on live television.

"And the results are in!" Georgina cried. "By an overwhelming margin . . . Camp Star!"

Across the stage, the Star campers were on their feet, cheering and screaming. Mitchie couldn't believe it. They'd put on the best performance ever, but it hadn't been enough. She felt tears slipping down her cheeks and her breath caught in her throat.

"Yes! Yes!" Luke exclaimed, punching the air and pointing over at the Camp Rockers in triumph. Tess was definitely happy, but she had the decency to shoot a mournful glance over to Mitchie, Ella, and Peggy.

Mitchie allowed her mom to give her a consoling hug. She felt devastated, but she joined the other Camp Rockers in congratulating Camp Star on their victory.

Then Brown rounded up his disappointed campers, and they paddled quietly back to the other side of the lake.

CHAPTER 12

Sitting on the Camp Rock beach at night with her best friends around the fire pit, listening to Nate strum his guitar, was normally one of Mitchie's favorite things to do.

But not tonight. Tonight the mood was somber. No one sang. Or talked. Mitchie stood at the flagpole with Shane. They were lowering the camp flag.

"I was thinking about keeping it as a souvenir,"

Mitchie said sadly, folding the flag.

Shane sighed. "I can't believe we lost."

"I guess every song can't be a hit," Mitchie said. "Didn't you tell me that? But that doesn't mean we should stop singing."

Shane looked at her, his brown eyes tender.

"I'm really sorry we didn't get to spend more time together," Mitchie said sadly. The summer had gone by so fast.

"Hey, the whole reason I came here this summer—" Shane began.

"Was to get to know me better," Mitchie finished, smiling.

"And I definitely learned everything I needed to know," Shane said quietly, leaning over to kiss her.

Nothing could make up for Camp Rock's loss to Camp Star. But being kissed by Shane Gray sure came close.

Holding hands, they walked back to the campfire. And as Nate continued to play his guitar, Shane started to sing. Soon Mitchie joined in, harmonizing. Then more Camp Rockers picked up the melody. Hearing all their voices blending together, singing about the incredible summer they'd had, made the disappointment a little easier to bear.

After all, they had had a fantastic summer. And to be there all together, well, there was nothing better.

"Look! What's that?" Trevor exclaimed. He pointed into the distance.

Dozens of lights were floating on the lake. As Mitchie squinted, trying to figure out what she was seeing, she realized the lights were lanterns. Some Star campers were coming over in rowboats and canoes, tying them to the dock and walking toward the campfire. Tess and Dana were leading the group.

What do they want? Mitchie wondered. She knew her fellow campers were wondering the same thing.

"Hi," Tess said. "We saw the fire. . . . "

"We really don't get to do this kind of thing,"

Dana added, gesturing around the group.

"So . . . do you think there's room for some of us?" Tess asked. Mitchie didn't miss the glimmer of hope and regret in Tess's voice.

Brown's voice was welcoming. "There's always room."

The Camp Rockers scooted over to make room for the Star campers.

"If it's okay with you, I'd like to come back to Camp Rock next summer," Tess blurted out to Brown.

From around the campfire, other voices chimed in. "I already called my parents and told them that I want to come here instead next summer," one Camp Star girl was saying.

"Are there any openings left?" a Camp Star boy was asking. "I wanna come, too."

Mitchie blinked in surprise as her mom came running up to the campfire from the main building. She was waving a phone in her hand. "Could I get a little help in here? The phones are going crazy!" Lots of aspiring rockers who had seen the TV broadcast wanted to sign up for spots at Camp Rock.

"Please!" exclaimed yet another Camp Star girl. "Can you at least put us on a list or something? This place is so much more fun."

Brown caught Mitchie's eye, and she beamed back at him. Maybe they hadn't lost the showdown after all.

Brown grinned at the Star campers. "I'm sure we can work something out," he told them as the Camp Rockers started to sing once more. The Star campers joined in and clapped along with the music.

They sang about being together, and how that was all that mattered. Mitchie looked over at Shane and knew that he agreed wholeheartedly.

Her second summer at Camp Rock had been completely different than what she had imagined it would be . . . and in the end, better than she could have ever dreamed. She had her friends, she had a great boyfriend, and she had her music.

Her life was like Camp Rock . . . it rocked!